# I'm Not Moving, Mama!

*Nancy White Carlstrom*

*illustrated by* Thor Wickstrom

**ALADDIN PAPERBACKS**

First Aladdin Paperbacks edition November 1999

Aladdin Paperbacks
An imprint of Simon & Schuster
Children's Publishing Division
1230 Avenue of the Americas
New York, NY 10020

The text for this book was set in 16 point Breughel 55.
The illustrations were rendered in pen and ink and watercolor.

Printed and bound in Hong Kong
10 9 8 7 6 5 4 3

The Library of Congress has cataloged the hardcover edition of this book as follows:

Carlstrom, Nancy White. I'm not moving, Mama!/ by Nancy White Carstrom;
illustrated by Thor Wickstrom.—1st American ed.    p.    cm.
Summary: Mama and child discuss the family's upcoming move to a new house
and the reasons why she does not wish to leave the child behind.
ISBN 0-02-717286-4 (hc.)
[1. Moving. Household—Fiction.  2. Mother and child—Fiction.]
I. Wickstrom, Thor, ill.  II. Title.
PZ7.C21684Iam   1990   [E]—dc20   89-38151   CIP   AC
ISBN 0-689-82881-0 (Aladdin pbk.)

For the Olsons
Wendy, Mark, Annie, and Peter
— N.W.C.


For my mother
— T.W.

You can take my bright green dinosaur.
But I'm not moving, Mama!

I'll sit here on the window seat
and watch the sun sit down in the sky.

But the sun comes, too,
and we couldn't paint the clouds pink without you.

You can take my checkers game.
But I'm not moving, Mama!

I'll be in my best hiding place
waiting for you to count to ten.

But there will be another hiding place,
and I will always find you.

You can take my monster toothbrush.
But I'm not moving, Mama!

I'll stand here at the mirror wiggling my loose tooth.

But there will be another mirror,
and we couldn't make funny faces without you.

You can take my building blocks.
But I'm not moving, Mama!

I'll be in the backyard
talking to the birds who live in the house we made.

But there will be more birds,
and we need you to feed them.

You can take my two-wheeler.
But I'm not moving, Mama!

I'll be in the climbing tree
looking through the leaves.

But there will be another climbing tree,
and we'll need you to get the kite out.

You can take my books.
Well, most of them.
But I'm not moving, Mama!

I'll be in the secret corner reading all by myself.

But there will be another secret corner,
and if you stay here, you will always be by yourself.
We would miss you.

You can take my motorcycle poster.
But I'm not moving, Mama!

I'll be in my room with the star window
still looking out tonight.

But the stars come, too,
and we couldn't get to sleep without you.

You can take my black boots.
But I'm not moving, Mama!

I'll be on my long rope swing
trying to touch the fence.

But there will be another swing,
and I can't open the gate without you.

You can make me go.
But I don't like moving, Mama!

I don't either.
But the best part
is not leaving you behind.

We'll remember the star window and the climbing tree,
the long rope swing and the sunset seat.

Someday, we'll say, "Remember how good it was to live in that old place."

*But it's better being all together in someplace new.*